GROUNDSEL

FERGUS HALL

JONATHAN CAPE
THIRTY BEDFORD SQUARE LONDON

OVER TO THE WEST, beyond the Mulberry Hills lie the three counties of Wookey Hollow, surrounded by a thick briar wood. No one had ever managed to penetrate more than a few yards into this forest; Father Time himself was no exception.

Many years ago he travelled the world, setting clocks in motion and regulating the seasons of the year. At last he came to the edge of the tangled woods. "Impossible to get through there," he murmured, "I'll have to go the long way round; Wookey Hollow must wait."

Of course he really meant to return, but somehow there always seemed to be more important business on hand. Eventually he forgot all about it.

THUS IT WAS that in Wookey Hollow the tick of a clock was never heard; time stood still at Summer and no one seemed to grow much older. The air was particularly mild and the fruits and flowers were unusually large. The ground rose gradually to a hill which overlooked the whole countryside. At its summit stood the strangest building imaginable, looking more like a greenhouse than a place in which to live. This was the home of Groundsel the gardener, who had the whole of Wookey Hollow in his keeping.

GROUNDSEL WAS FAMOUS for his wonderful ability to grow things. It was well known that both his thumbs were green and that he spent a lot of time talking to seedlings. Some spiteful folk said he looked rather "plantish" himself. In fact, the mild climate made his work very easy. Trimming the hedges and watering the plants were his main occupations.

E FLEW FARTHER NORTH than he had ever ventured before. Eventually the oceans disappeared and he was surrounded by darkness, relieved only by the occasional snowflake.

At last he arrived in the freezing wastes where Winter dwells and, hopping boldly on to her outstretched hand, he said,

"There is a land to the south-west which you have never visited."

"Foolish bird," she replied, "how can that be?"

Maggot-Pie explained that Father Time had forgotten about Wookey Hollow, with the result that it was always Summer-time there.

"Those poor plants go on blooming all year round. They deserve a rest, like anyone else," he concluded.

At this, Winter ordered Maggot-Pie to fly home:

"This state of affairs must be corrected. My Autumn winds will speed you on your way. In return you must guide my trusty servant Jack to Wookey Hollow."

Jack Frost hopped on Maggot-Pie's back and with the help of the following winds, they reached the three counties in no time.

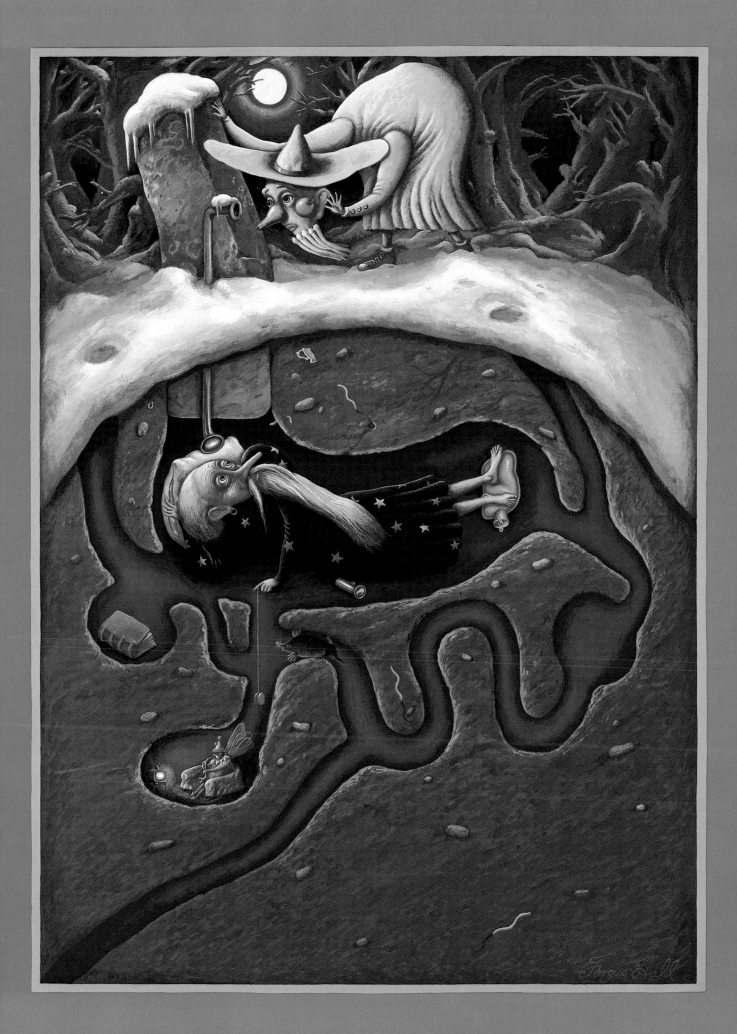

E HAD NO IDEA where to start searching for Time, and besides he was much too tired. Instead, he relit the fire and sat gazing into the orange flames. Suddenly he remembered what Merlin had said about the sun melting the frost.

"Might as well try something else before setting out on another wild goose chase," he thought.

He stoked the fire until it roared in the chimney, then closed the windows tight and blocked up every crack and cranny in the house. He waited. The room grew hotter and hotter. At last he heard the sharp crunch of approaching footsteps and Jack stepped inside. Groundsel leapt up and locked the door.

"Got you!" he cried. "Now you're going to stay here until you melt clean away, Jack."

Jack looked about him apprehensively. Already a drip was forming on the end of his nose. He had to do something quickly. In one bound he was at the fireside.

"You don't get rid of me so easily, Groundsel. See you soon," he called and leapt straight up the chimney, dislodging soot and snow and all manner of rubbish as he went.